Santa Clawziz Comin-2-Town

Michael Carter Griffin

BENNETT
MEDIA & MARKETING

Santa Clawziz Comin-2-Town

Bennett books may be ordered through booksellers or by contacting:

Bennett Media and Marketing
1603 Capitol Ave., Suite 310 A233
Cheyenne, WY 82001
www.thebennettmediaandmarketing.com
Phone: 1-307-202-9292

ISBN
978-1-957114-92-7 (Paperback)
978-1-957114-93-4 (eBook)

Dedicated to Tilly and Oliver.
You are both Awesome + Amazing = Awesumazing.
(Yes - that's a word - I made it up).
We Love You a Buhzillion Guhzillion.

hey everybody - watcha gonna do -
there's a man named santa -
he be lookin for you

he left the North Pole singin HoHoHo -
now he's flyin thru the air like uh UFO

he be comin down the chimney-he be
makin some noise-singin Merry Little
Christmas to duh girls and duh boys
ridin dat sleigh - bringin all the presents -
flyin thru the sky like uh 747

you know you bettuh watch out - you know
you bettuh not cry

yuh bettuh not pout like a little bitty cry
baby and I'm tellin everybody why

santa clawziz comin 2 town - santa clawziz
flyin all around
everybody gotta get the news around -
everybody yell it out loud

he's lean - he's mean - he's duh best yu
evuh seen - he's a one man reindeer flyin
machine

V2

he be flyin to the west – he be flyin to the east – he be flyin all over – mr santa iz a beast

he's a force like darth vaduh – see yuh latuh alligatuh – flyin straight up like a one-way elevatuh

you know mizzez clawz gonna start duh
celebration – santa knows it's all about duh
jingelization

elves are laughin – reindeer prancin –
everybody's up at duh north pole dancing
you know santuz makin dat list – you know
santuz checkin it twice

santa says we should try to be nice, so let
your hearts shine like Christmas lights

santa clawziz comin 2 town – santa clawziz
flyin all around

santuz on a one-night ride – santuz
everywhere; he's worldwide

santa and the reindeer - flyin thru the snow

with the 4 elf riders - eeny, meeny, miney, mo

santa he couldn't bring the elf on a shelf
he's got phobia phobia - the fear of fear itself

X's and O's - hugs and kisses - they call him
lucky charms - he's magically delicious
bueanus notchus - a tiger he's ferocious -
he's super-kaluh-frajuh-listik-expee-aluh-
doshus

santa sees you when yuh sleepin - santa
knows when you're awake
santa knows when you been bad or good -
he's got security cameras all over duh place

santa clawziz comin 2 town - santa clawziz
flyin all around
santa - you can hear him jingle - everybody
calls him kris kringle

santa - he be flyin so free - singin pour
some suguh on me

santa waves to everybody as he's flyin
outta sight
Merry Christmas to all, and to all - Sy-uh-
nahrah

The End

Believe in the Miracle
You Already Are
Believe in the Miracle
You are Meant to Become

Merry Christmas

Love Never Ending

Inside my heart, I see your smile tonight
Love Never Ending - We're Walking in the Light
Your heart cries softly - tears we will remember
Gentle whispers calling out - a love that lasts forever

The sky can be a canvas - painted white and gray
The storm is a symphony - the music is the rain
The clouds roll back, and we'll see heaven's light shine through
Feel the breeze upon your face, and remember - I will always be with you

In my heart, you will always stay
The morning sun - I hold you every day
In your heart, I will always be
The midnight sky - the brightest star you'll see

Close your eyes, and look beyond the world we see
Now - Always - Forever - I hold you close to me
You'll find me in the sunset - we'll paint the sky so bright
Our Love is Never Ending - We're Walking in the Light

These words point to five gifts that carry us every day, and help us to carry others.
- Strength, Courage, Faith, Hope - All surrounded by the greatest gift we can ever receive, and the most powerful gift we can ever give - LOVE!

I will stand with you
I will stand beside you
I'm standing right beside you - Now - Always - Forever
Love Never Ending - We're Walking in the Light